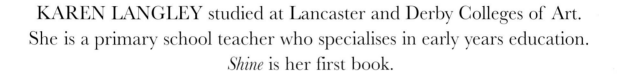

KAREN LANGLEY studied at Lancaster and Derby Colleges of Art.
She is a primary school teacher who specialises in early years education.
Shine is her first book.

Jonathan Langley studied at the Liverpool College of Art
and the Central School of Art and Design.
A hugely successful author and illustrator, his children's books
have sold over a million copies throughout the world.
His first book for Frances Lincoln was *Missing!*

Karen and Jonathan live in the Lake District with their children.

For my three stars and Baby Billy – *K.L.*
For John and Pamela – *J.L.*

Shine copyright © Frances Lincoln Limited 2002
Text copyright © Karen Langley 2002
Illustrations copyright © Jonathan Langley 2002

First published in Great Britain in 2002 by
Frances Lincoln Limited, 4 Torriano Mews,
Torriano Avenue, London NW5 2RZ
www.franceslincoln.com

First paperback edition 2003

British Library Cataloguing in Publication Data available on request

ISBN 0-7112-1943-5 HB
ISBN 0-7112 2116-2 PB

Printed in Singapore

3 5 7 9 8 6 4

SHINE

Karen and Jonathan Langley

FRANCES LINCOLN

"Dad! Dad! I'm a star in the School Play," said Jimmy.
"I've got to shine. Will you come and see me?"

"You'll have to practise hard," said Dad.
"I will come and watch you, as long as I'm not called out."

Just then the telephone rang.

"Here we go again," said Dad. "Run upstairs and get ready for bed, and I'll come and say goodnight before I go."

Jimmy washed his face, cleaned his teeth and brushed his hair.

"Am I shining, Dad?" said Jimmy.
"You're beginning to sparkle," said Dad.

Sometimes Dad worked at night when it was dark,

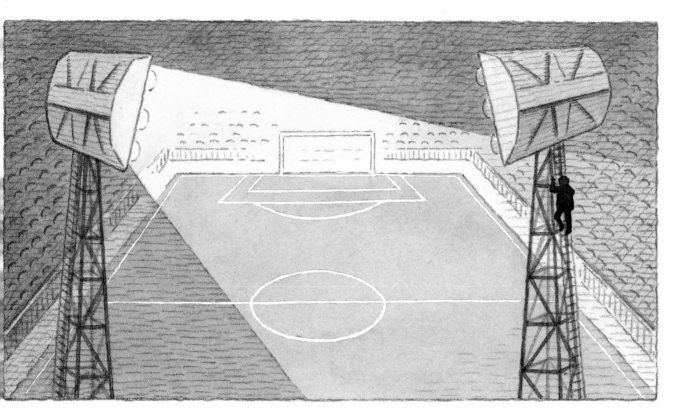

so Nana put Jimmy to bed.

Next day the play rehearsals began.
Every day the children practised.

Every day Jimmy practised shining.

"Am I shining, Dad?" asked Jimmy.
"Yes, you're glimmering tonight," said Dad.

"I hope you can come and see me, Dad,"
said Jimmy.

The day of the show came.
 "Will you come and see me, Dad?" asked Jimmy.

"I'll do my very best, Jimmy," said Dad, as he left
the house and went out into the darkness with his toolbox.
"It starts at 7 o'clock!" Jimmy shouted after him.

Jimmy went back to school after tea. It was very dark.

"What's in the bag?" asked Nana.

"Oh, just some stuff I need for the play," replied Jimmy.

There were lots of people in the hall at school.

Jimmy couldn't see his Dad.

'I hope Dad comes to see me shine,' he thought.

'I hope Dad comes to see me shine.'

'I hope he comes.'

'I'm sure he'll be here soon.'

'Where's my Dad?'

The play began.

The curtains swished.

The donkey bumped.

The sheep shoved.

The shepherds stumbled.

The angels giggled.

The kings sneezed.

Mary, Joseph and the baby Jesus snuggled.

It was nearly the end. Time for Jimmy the Star to travel across the stage and stand next to baby Jesus.

'Where's my Dad?' thought Jimmy, looking out into the audience.

Suddenly through the sea of faces Jimmy saw his Dad.
His face seemed to be shining like a light out of the
crowd, smiling at him.

Jimmy stood on his box holding the star up high

and he smiled and smiled and smiled.

After the show, Jimmy and Dad walked home together.
"Did I shine, Dad?" asked Jimmy.

"You shone, Jimmy," said Dad. "You shone bright enough to light up even the darkest of skies."